FT. BRAGG BRANCH LIBRARY

Mendocino County Library

OCT 1 3 2013

D0819741

To Bob —

    We thought of you because this book is about a father — and you had a special relationship with yours and with your own children.

        Love,

           Barbara & Clarence

Christmas 1987

WITHDRAWN

KITE FLIER

Dennis Haseley   illustrations by David Wiesner

Four Winds Press · New York   Collier Macmillan Publishers · London

Text copyright © 1986 by Dennis Haseley
Illustrations copyright © 1986 by David Wiesner
All rights reserved. No part of this book may be reproduced or
transmitted in any form or by any means, electronic or mechanical, including
photocopying, recording, or by any information storage and retrieval
system, without permission in writing from the Publisher.
Four Winds Press
Macmillan Publishing Company
866 Third Avenue, New York, NY 10022
Collier Macmillan Canada, Inc.
Printed and bound in Japan
First American Edition

10 9 8 7 6 5 4 3 2 1

The text of this book is set in 14 pt. ITC Cheltenham Light Condensed.
The illustrations are rendered in watercolor.
Library of Congress Cataloging-in-Publication Data
Haseley, Dennis.
Kite flier.
Summary: A father sends his magnificent kites
soaring through the sky to express his feelings
toward his restless son.
[1. Kites—Fiction. 2. Fathers and sons—Fiction]
I. Wiesner, David, ill. II. Title.
PZ7.H2688Ki   1986   [E]   86-38
ISBN 0-02-743110-X

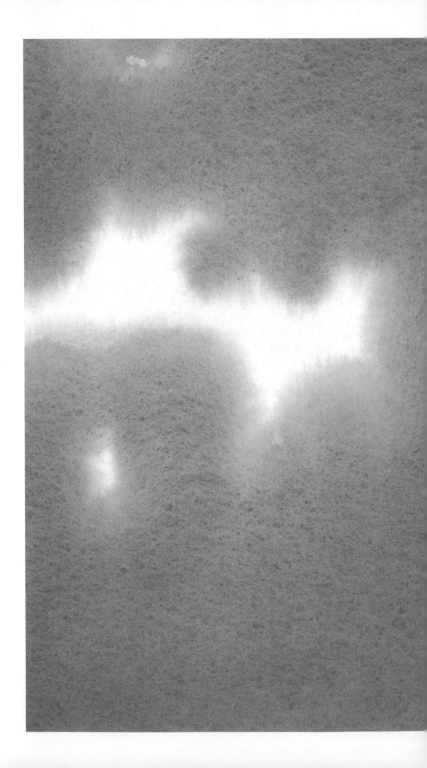

For Claudia   —D.H.

For Mike   —D.W.

My father told me
that when he was young
he had traveled far from his home.
Finally he came to a house
on a hill overlooking a village.
He learned the trade of
stonework, while above him the clouds
floated, like silk.

Then he married
the beautiful daughter of a farmer
and he began to fly kites.

He made kites of paper and wood
that looked like crickets
and cats, and a heron kite
made of white silk.
He flew them while my mother watched.
Then, like a fisherman, he reeled them in,
and while she laughed,
he showed her what he'd caught.

The children of the village
watched our house on the hill
and the kites flying overhead, and they said,
"Kite Flier is a wizard
and can fly anything,
even the stones he sets during the day."
He laughed when he heard this.
He knew it was his heart that was flying.

After they were married for a time
my mother gave birth to me
and became sick
and died.

And then Kite Flier
made no kites.

But one day
a scrap of silk
from an old heron kite
caught in the wind
and flew over my cradle.
My father heard me laugh.

So he started making kites for me.

"Watch," he said, as I lay on a blanket.
And beneath a crescent moon
my father flew a kite
that looked like the crescent moon.
"And there!" he shouted,
and in a field of flowers
he flew a kite like a blowing flower
that I chased with my first steps.

When the children in the village
saw the shapes flying,
they came to our door and said,
"Kite Flier, sell us your kites."
He only shook his head and smiled.

As I grew older
my father flew other kites.
The day I learned to swim
he launched the paper
body of a fish
with my proud head on it,
and I laughed to see it
skim and dive.

When I fell from a tree
and twisted my leg,
he carried me home
and sat with me all night.
In the sky above us
flew the gentle face of a woman.
And the day I killed a rabbit
with a stone,
he angrily sent me back to our house,
and later I saw him fly a kite
that flashed like lightning
in the sky.

Like a fisherman
who never lost a catch,
he reeled in each kite
and saved it.
Later he taught me to build one.
It was small and square
and when I ran with it,
it kicked like a puppy
before it rose.

I grew taller and stronger
and played in the village with the other boys,
who were no longer so interested in kites.
As I spent less time with my father,
he dreamed up kites I would love,
kites of jackknives and dragons and masks,
kites that skipped across the sky
as I ran, and two fighter kites,
one that always chased the other.

One day, my father launched a silver kite
that rose and rose,
and I closed my eyes and
pretended I was soaring.
I could see so far,
and he was so small on the ground beneath me.

Filled with faraway thoughts,
I sat and gazed at the road
or drew with a stick in the dirt.
My father flew kites of blue and purple streamers
that circled over me,
and I would look at them sometimes,
so pale they were almost invisible.

Finally, there came a day
when all the kites my father flew
could not make me smile or speak,
so faraway were my thoughts.

And I came to my father and said
that I was now a young man
and wished to go and see
the world away from my home.

"No, you must stay," said my father
in a voice as heavy as a rock.
I could see the colors of the kites
behind him start to run, but I said,
"I am sorry, I must travel now
as you did
when you were a young man."

That night,
my father and I
set to work.

We gathered those kites he had built
for my mother and for me,
cricket kites, kites like moons,
like ships and cats,
and for days and days he worked,
carefully sewing the silk, gluing the
bright paper, while I held and bent
the thin wood.

He worked with all his craft
and I with all my strength
until we built a huge kite.

On a windy morning,
he carried it from our house
and I walked behind, watching as he bent
beneath a magnificent kite
in the shape of a bird.
It was streaked with the colors
of sky and stone,
and its wings, when they caught
the morning sun, glowed
with the colors of flames.
As I helped him lift it into
the wind, those wings
fanned wide, and its tail of
silk streamed out like clouds.
We watched that wild bird rise above us,
and when I caught a glimpse of its face,
it looked like a human face
with eyes
faraway like stars.

Together, we
held tightly to the line
as the bird dove and tossed.
We held on as it tugged in the morning wind
and then, watching as it soared in the clear air,
first I
and then he
let the string go.
As the kite disappeared into the sky,
my father gave a cry.

Then I walked down the hill
to the road.
And he turned
and walked toward the village.

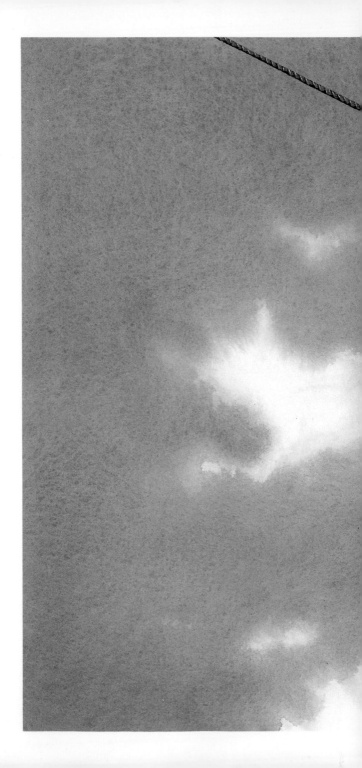

I have not seen my father in a long time.
But I know that always
on the first strong wind of the year
each of us climbs a hill
and sets a kite
free.